Endorsements

In *Little Sprout Says Yes!* by Jennifer E. Tirrell we see again God's gentle and welcoming hand. This colorful little book is an embracing gift to youth everywhere.

Leo Hindery, Jr., Philanthropist
Author, *It Takes a CEO: It's Time to Lead with Integrity*

Little Sprout Says Yes! will grab your child's attention from the beginning and never let go. Children will identify with Little Sprout as he searches the farm to see where he belongs and who he can trust. Relating Sprout's adoption to our adoption in God's kingdom will help your child understand God's acceptance and love for us all as we say, "Yes" to Him and are adopted by our Heavenly Father.

Linda Summerford
Author, *The Glider*

Copyright © 2025 Jennifer E. Tirrell

Little Sprout Says Yes!

Written by Jennifer E. Tirrell
Illustrated by Lissette Blanco

ISBN: 978-1-963377-32-3 (paperback)
ISBN: 978-1-963377-38-5 (hardcover)

Published by Abundance Books, LLC
Kalamazoo, MI

www.abundance-books.com

Printed in the United States of America

10 9 8 7 6 5 3 2 1

All rights reserved. No part of this publication may be reproduced, distributed, or transmitted in any form or by any means, including photocopying, recording, or other electronic or mechanical methods, without the prior written permission of the publisher, except in the case of brief quotations embodied in critical reviews and certain other noncommercial uses permitted by copyright law.

Scriptures taken from the HOLY BIBLE, NEW LIVING TRANSLATION, Copyright© 1996, 2004, 2007 by Tyndale House Foundation. Used by permission of Tyndale House Publishers, Inc., Carol Stream, Illinois 60188. All rights reserved. Used by permission.

This book is given with love

_____

_____

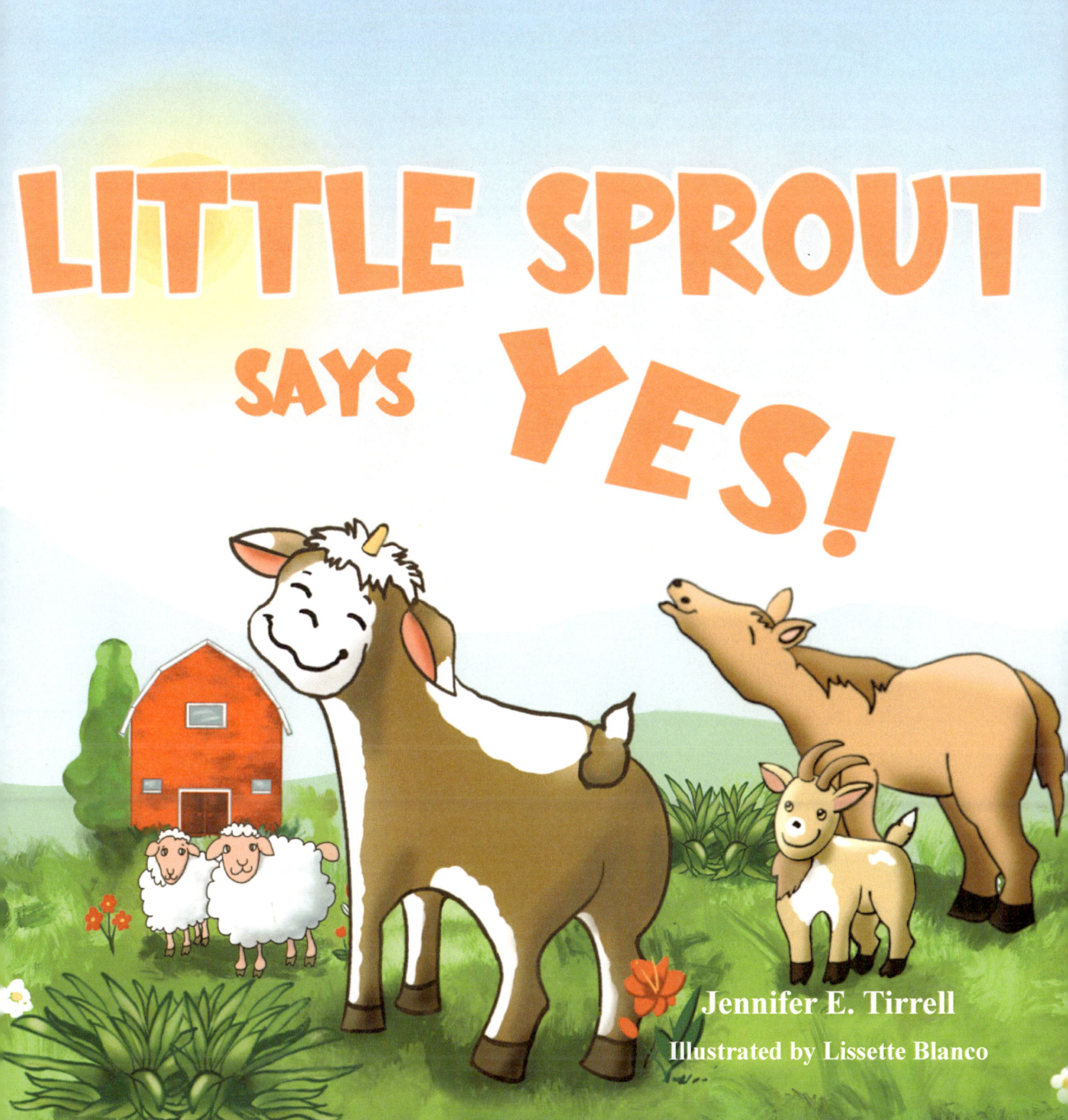

A Note from Jennifer

In 1967, I was kinship adopted by my sister and brother-in-law. They took me in after I became an orphan at three years of age. I needed a home, and they had one to share. Suddenly, my family included a new mom and dad and more brothers and sisters. Even in this stable and loving environment, I often felt confused. My new parents brought me to church. In the family of God, I found belonging and began to thrive.

Little Sprout's story is similar to mine. He lives on a children's discipleship farm in North Carolina. Born a runt, and trimmed of his horns, Little Sprout managed to grow to full size after being adopted and loved by his Glory Hill Farm (gloryhillfarm.org) family. Against the odds, he even grew one little horn.

God initiated adoption when He "decided in advance to adopt us into his own family by bringing us to himself through Jesus Christ." (Ephesians 1:5)

You can be adopted, too! Just ask God.

Dedication

Little Sprout Says Yes!
is dedicated to my grandchildren
—my little warriors for Christ.

E. J. Nowak IV, Gabriel Michael Havanka,
Celine Elise Bakes, and Griffin Judah Havanka.

One sunny springtime day,
three baby goats were born.
One goat was very tiny,
and he only had one horn.

The bigger goats were very fast.
The bigger goats were strong.
The little goat with one horn wondered,
Where do I belong?

Some folks arrived at the farm one day.
They woke him from a rest.
"We're here to buy two goats," they said.
"We only want the best!"

"There are three goats out in the field,
 but one's a little runt.

Runts require extra work,
to really be quite blunt."

The big goats reared and locked their horns.
The one-horned goat stayed still.
His brothers put on quite a show—
they kicked and jumped with skill.

"We'll take those two," the people said. "That little sprout looks weak."

Is that my name? thought Little Sprout, alone and very meek.

The truck revved up its engine and left in a cloud of dust.

Little Sprout looked around the farm. Was there no one he could trust?

A green frog croaked in a nearby pond,
and a rooster sang "Good Day!"

"Will you be my family?" he asked the cows,
chewing their morning cud.
"You're not like us, so move along.
Try that pig over there in the mud."

The next day, another truck arrived.
The animals asked, "Why?"

"I heard you have a goat for sale,
so I thought I'd drop on by."

Finishing his banana,
the farmer threw down its peel.
"We have one that needs adoption,
but he's small and not ideal."

"That's just fine," the lady said.
God loves us all, you see.
He wants to adopt each one of us
into his family tree."

Little Sprout jumped very high.
The lady was impressed.
He slipped on the banana peel.
Oh my! What a mess.

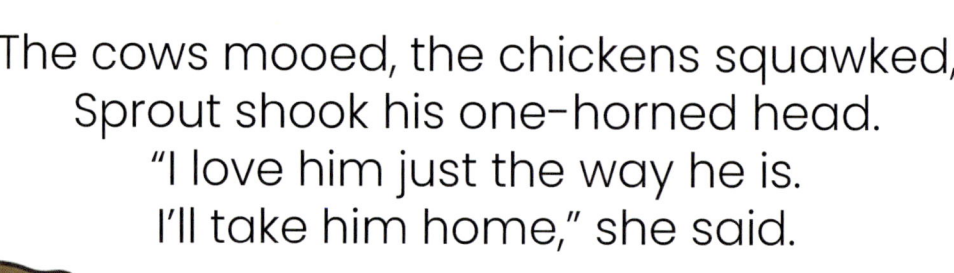

The cows mooed, the chickens squawked,
Sprout shook his one-horned head.
"I love him just the way he is.
I'll take him home," she said.

God designed a special plan
to help us find our way.
We all belong to Him, you see.
He leads us day by day.

Jesus paid the price for us.
There's no need to jump so high.
Just say, "Thank you, Jesus!"
and you'll feel like you can fly!

Fur, skin, or fluffy fleeces,
brown, black, green, blue or white—
we're created for His pleasure,
and all perfect in His sight.

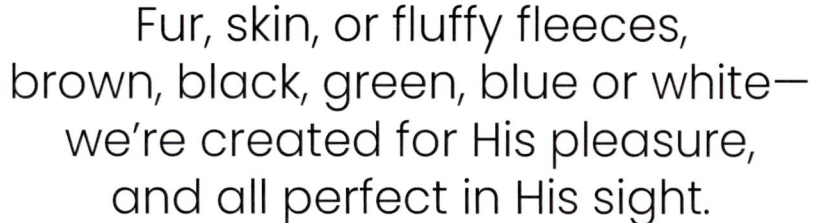

Each precious soul, uniquely made,
is given the same option.
Say "Yes!" to Him, and you will find
true family by adoption!

Little Sprout bleated "Yes!" with joy.
He joined the goats and sheep,
the chickens, horses, and the pigs—
and chicks who chirp, "Peep! Peep!"

Love God and love our neighbors,
that's all we have to do,
to have a true forever home
and a family through and through.

Read on to find pictures of the real Little Sprout!
You can meet him in person!
Check out gloryhillfarm.org.

Goats are ruminants. They are always chewing, chewing, chewing!

All wrapped up for Jesus!

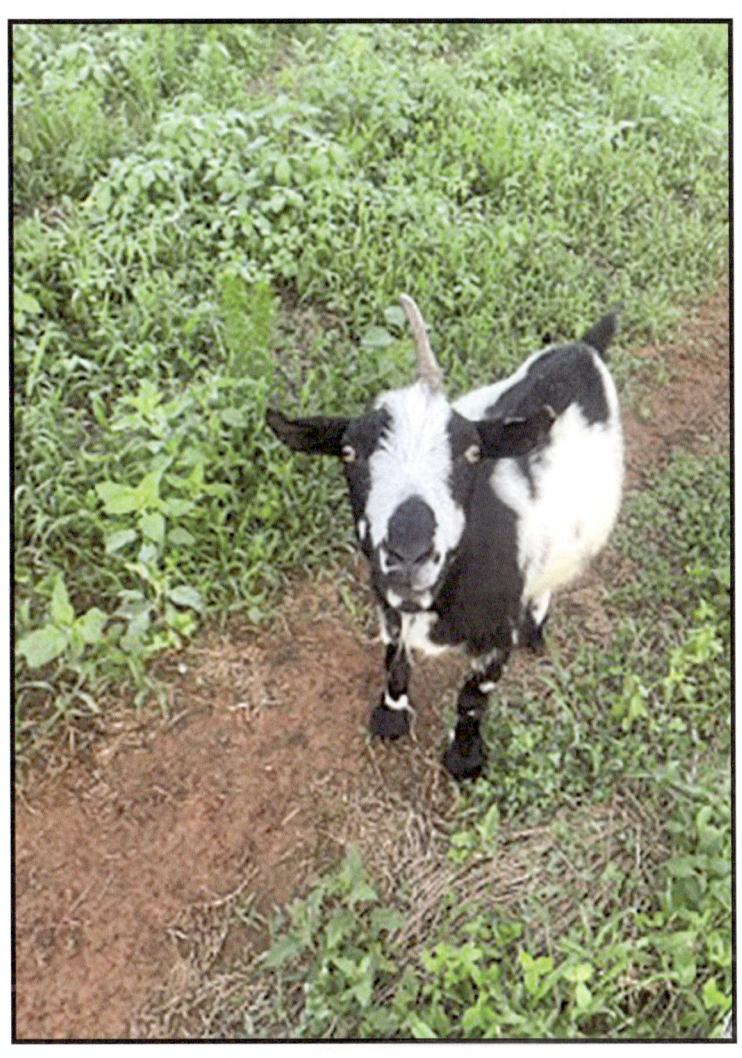

Little Sprout loves fresh, green forage to eat!

Rusty the Quarter Horse says, "Yes!" to Little Sprout sharing his hay.

"My turn next!"

"Look! I can do it!"

Little Sprout with his friend Liberty and her twins, Sugar and Spice.

About the Author

Writing flows from Jennifer E. Tirrell's heart and mind as easily as water over stones in a creek bed. Her passion is to draw children and young adults to God in ways she benefited as an orphaned child—through simply told, stimulating stories with intriguing faith foundations. Find her at writingwithjet.com, at the beach, or helping out at Little Sprout's forever home, Glory Hill Farm in Monroe, North Carolina.

About the Illustrator

Lissette Blanco is a Christian children's book illustrator with a background in fine arts and prophetic painting. Deeply rooted in her faith and love for ministry, Lissette combines her artistic gifts with her passion for storytelling, creating heartwarming illustrations that inspire and delight young readers. She began writing and illustrating books for her grandchildren, blending creativity and faith to share God's love with future generations. Born and raised in Guatemala, she now lives in the United States, where she continues her ministry and artistic work.

www.ingramcontent.com/pod-product-compliance
Lightning Source LLC
Chambersburg PA
CBRC092042170125
20549CB00009B/22